Starry Forest Books, Inc. • P.O. Box 1797, 217 East 70th Street, New York, NY 10021 • Starry Forest® is a registered trademark of Starry Forest Books, Inc. • Text and Illustrations © 2020 by Starry Forest Books, Inc. • This 2020 edition published by Starry Forest Books, Inc. • All rights reserved. No part of this publication may be reproduced, stored in a retrieval system, or transmitted in any form or by any means (including electronic, mechanical, photocopying, recording, or otherwise) without prior written permission from the publisher. • ISBN 978-1-946260-30-7 • Manufactured in Huizhou City, Guangdong Province, China • Lot #: 2 4 6 8 10 9 7 5 3 1 • 04/20

CLASSIC STORIES

The Three Musketeers

Alexandre Dumas

retold by Saviour Pirotta

illustrated by John Manders

Starry Forest Books

D'Artagnan

D'Artagnan was headed to Paris. He had little money in his pocket. But he did have a letter of introduction that his father had written to Mr. Treville, the captain of the king's guards, the Musketeers. All his life, d'Artagnan had dreamed of being a Musketeer: the finest, most noble soldiers in France. Now he was on his way.

D'Artagnan stopped at an inn just outside Paris.

"Look at that horse!" guffawed a nobleman with a scar on his head. "It's as yellow as a buttercup."

"No man laughs at my horse," cried d'Artagnan. He whipped out his sword but one of the nobleman's servants struck him on the head with a shovel.

D'Artagnan woke. He heard the nobleman saying, "Hurry to England, Milady de Winter. You know what Cardinal Richelieu wants you to do."

"Yes, Comte de Rochfort," answered the lady.

They left. D'Artagnan was about to leave, too. He reached in his pocket to pay the innkeeper, and realized: *Comte de Rochefort stole my letter!*

D'Artagnan went straight to Mr. Treville in Paris. "I want to be
a Musketeer," he said. "But a scoundrel stole my letter of introduction
to you."

"With or without a letter, you must prove yourself worthy," said
Mr. Treville. "Only then can you become a Musketeer."

"Thank you, sir," cried d'Artagnan.

Suddenly, three magnificent Musketeers swept in. D'Artagnan bowed, awed by these men, his heroes!

"Athos, Porthos, Aramis," said Mr. Treville. "Meet d'Artagnan. He wants to be a Musketeer."

The three men smiled. "We shall soon see if he is worthy," said Aramis.

"I'll soon prove that I am!" declared d'Artagnan.

But things didn't go as well as he'd hoped.

He knocked Athos's hat into a puddle.

"I challenge you to a duel at noon!" said Athos.

He smeared mud on Porthos's boot.

"I challenge you to a duel at one o'clock!" said Porthos.

He spooked Aramis's horse.

"I challenge you to a duel at two o'clock!" said Aramis.

At noon, Athos and d'Artagnan drew their swords. Suddenly Cardinal Richelieu's guards galloped up. The cardinal was the most powerful man in France after the king. He had his own guards, who hated the Musketeers.

"Duelling on the streets is against the law," shouted their captain. "You Musketeers are all under arrest."

"You'll have to catch us first," cried Aramis.

D'Artagnan joined in the fight with relish, brandishing his sword with such force that the guards soon fled, fearing for their lives.

"You are indeed brave, young d'Artagnan!" said Aramis. "Forget the duels. You can be our friend."

A young woman named Constance came to see d'Artagnan. "The queen needs your help," said Constance. "The king gave her a necklace with twelve diamonds in it. Evil Cardinal Richelieu found out that she gave it away to her friend, the Duke of Buckingham, an enemy of the king."

"Go to London and give the duke this letter," said Constance.
"Bring the necklace back before the ball."

"I will leave at once," said d'Artagnan, tucking the letter in his pocket.

D'Artagnan explained the queen's problem to Athos, Porthos, and Aramis.
"Will you help me get the necklace?" he asked. "It will be dangerous."

"Of course we will help you!" said his three friends.

They drew their swords and put the tips together. "All for one, and one for all!"

Immediately, they left Paris, riding as fast as their horses could go, hurrying to reach the coast. There they would find a ship to carry them to England.

The four brave friends did not know that Cardinal Richelieu was plotting against them.

After a few hours of hard riding, they stopped at an inn. A stranger lumbered up to Porthos. "Let's drink a toast to Cardinal Richelieu," he said.

Porthos frowned. "I will drink only to the king!"

The stranger shoved Porthos, and then whipped out a knife. "Musketeer," he spat. "Fight me if you dare."

"Porthos," said Aramis. "We don't have time for this."

"I cannot back down from such a swine," said Porthos. "Let the battle begin!"

Aramis, Athos, and d'Artagnan had no choice. They had to fight, too.

Porthos was so badly wounded that they had to leave him behind at the inn.

Night fell. D'Artagnan, Athos, and Aramis rode into a deep valley.
Suddenly, hundreds of hissing arrows rained down on them. "It's an ambush!"
Athos shouted.

There was no way to fight back. They couldn't even see their attackers.

They rode on blindly. Then, *thwack*. "I'm hit!" cried Aramis.
An arrow stuck in his arm.

D'Artagnan pulled Aramis onto his horse. When they were safely
out of the valley, Aramis said, "I'm too weak to go on. Leave me."

But at a tavern, trouble awaited Athos and d'Artagnan. When Athos paid for their food, the landlord accused him, "You gave me counterfeit money!"

"That's a lie!" said Athos.

"Guards! Arrest this man!" shouted the landlord.

Suddenly, a guard grabbed Athos from behind. Another held a sword to his chest. Two guards came toward d'Artagnan, their swords drawn. "It's a trap!" Athos shouted. "Go!"

D'Artagnan bolted from the inn, leapt onto his horse, and rode off, leaving the guards in the dust.

As d'Artagnan neared the Port of Calais, his tired horse refused to take another step. Alone and weary, d'Artagnan trudged the rest of the way to the docks and boarded the ship that would take him to England.

The journey across the channel was stormy. Wind and waves tossed the ship around like a cork. When at last d'Artagnan landed in England, he rented a horse, rode to London, and found the Duke of Buckingham.

"Alas!" cried the duke when he read the queen's letter.
"Two of the diamonds were stolen. I believe Cardinal Richelieu ordered
Milady de Winter to steal them. He wants to shame the queen."

"The king will be furious if he sees diamonds are missing," said d'Artagnan. "You must replace them. But hurry. The ball is in five days."

For three anxious days, d'Artagnan and the duke stood over the jeweler at his bench, urging him to work faster. But the old man would not be rushed.

At last the diamonds were ready. D'Artagnan slipped them into a pouch and bade the duke goodbye.

"Thank you, d'Artagnan," said the duke. "I am in your debt. You have protected the queen's honor and mine as well. Think of me as a friend from now on."

D'Artagnan rushed back to Paris and went straight to the queen.

"You brought the diamonds!" said the queen. "Thank you!"

"Your majesty," said Constance. "The ball is beginning. We must go."

The queen took d'Artagnan's hand. "I will never forget your kindness," she said. Then she and Constance hurried off.

The king smiled, pleased to see the queen wearing the necklace.

Cardinal Richelieu was furious. *How did she get all twelve diamonds back?* he wondered.

D'Artagnan enjoyed the ball. But he enjoyed seeing the cardinal's displeasure even more!

The next day, Mr. Treville said, "D'Artagnan, you have proven your valor." D'Artagnan's chest swelled with pride as Mr. Treville signed an official document and said, "Now you are truly a Musketeer."

Athos, Porthos, and Aramis held up their swords, and d'Artagnan did, too.
Together they shouted:

"All for one, and one for all!"